Doodle Dog

Granny Doodle Day

Eric Seltzer

ALADDIN
New York London Toronto Sydney

ALADDIN PAPERBACKS

An imprint of Simon & Schuster Children's Publishing Division
1230 Avenue of the Americas, New York, NY 10020
Copyright © 2006 by Eric Seltzer
READY-TO-READ is a registered trademark of Simon & Schuster, Inc.
ALADDIN PAPERBACKS and colophon are
trademarks of Simon & Schuster, Inc.
Designed by Lisa Vega
The text of this book was set in CenturyOldst BT.
Manufactured in the United States of America
First Aladdin Paperbacks edition April 2006
2 4 6 8 10 9 7 5 3 1
Library of Congress Cataloging-in-Publication Data
Seltzer, Eric.
Granny Doodle day / by Eric Seltzer.
p. cm.
Summary: Three friends take a trip to visit Granny Doodle and
enjoy a Doodle Noodle, but not before fixing her wobbly table.
ISBN-13: 978-0-689-85911-3   ISBN-10: 0-689-85911-2
[1. Dogs—Fiction. 2. Bears—Fiction. 3. Grandmothers—Fiction.
4. Repairing—Fiction. 5. Stories in rhyme.] I. Title.
PZ8.3.S4665Gr 2005
[E]—dc22 2003011074

For Mike, Lori, Justin,
and Kit.
Thanks to Lisa Vega

A lazy day
to sit and stare.

I see a cloud.

It looks like Bear.

Another one
comes rolling by.

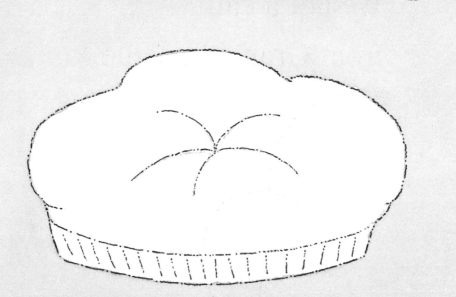

"Yum," says King.
"Apple pie!"

We get a call
from Granny Doodle.

"Would you like
a Doodle Noodle?"

King and I
drive far away.

We pass the beach

and sail the bay.

TO GRANNY DOODLE

We pick up Bear
along the way.

ART
TO GO

We smell something
with our noses.

I ♥ Honey

"Perfect. Granny loves pink roses."

5¢

She greets us
with hugs and smooches.

One for bears.

Two for pooches.

Granny says,
"Noodle eaters,

I need help!
My table teeters."

"Doodle here!"
I take some clay.

Now the table
does not sway.

Time to eat!
I lick my plate.

Then we find
a place to skate.

We take a swim,

play Ping-Pong,

then we have
a sing-a-long.

Back inside
I want a drink.

Gran pours grape juice
by the sink.

After juice
we plant the rose.

Then we take
a Doodle doze.

"Before you go,"

calls Granny Doodle,

"Take another
Doodle Noodle!"

We drive along
under the moon.
Days with Granny
end too soon.